Dear Oliver,

Thank you for your time & support.

Believe in yourself

Princess

Sydney Strong

S

What Makes

Me Different

By Jerry Carchi

Sydney

Princess Sydney Strong

What Makes Me Different

By

Jerry Carchi

Acknowledgment

This book could not have been written without the love and support of my wife Virginia Carchi. You are the wind in my sails and the beat in my heart. I would also like to thank all of my family and friends for being the Kingdom of people who help build a great foundation of love, laughter, and life for Sydney.

Dedication

This is dedicated to my daughter Sydney: You are the biggest inspiration and teacher in my life.

Mommy and I are so proud of you and so honored you chose us to be your parents.

Always stay the fighter that you are and the world will be yours.

This is a story about Princess Sydney Strong, a princess who is from a large Kingdom named Resilience.

It got its name by bouncing back from hurricane floods, attacks from other kingdoms, and earthquakes.

In this Kingdom the King and Queen were excited about the new baby coming into their lives.

All of the Kingdom was also excited.

Then came the day when Princess Sydney was born.

Of course the King and Queen wanted to see the baby right away. However, the doctor looked a little worried.

"What's wrong?" the King asked the doctor.

"Oh...nothing, your daughter looks just a bit different," said the doctor.

The King grew worried and asked, "What do you mean, does she have two eyes, one nose, one mouth, and two ears?

"Yes!" said the doctor.

"Well, out with it doctor!" exclaimed the King

"Well, she does have everything you said, it is just her eyes and head. Her eyes are very large and her head is not as round as it should be."

The King replied, "It doesn't matter she is our child and we will love her no matter what she looks like."

The doctor later explained to the King and Queen, "Princess Sydney has a Syndrome called "Extraordinary ME." This syndrome requires the princess to have surgeries to help her head and face."

The King and Queen were both scared and shocked, but knew they had to be strong for Princess Sydney and would need to help her along the way.

"Now what to do about the Kingdom?" wondered the King. The Queen replied, "We will wait until the princess is over her surgeries before we present her." They both felt they needed to protect her from the unwanted stares of the Kingdom.

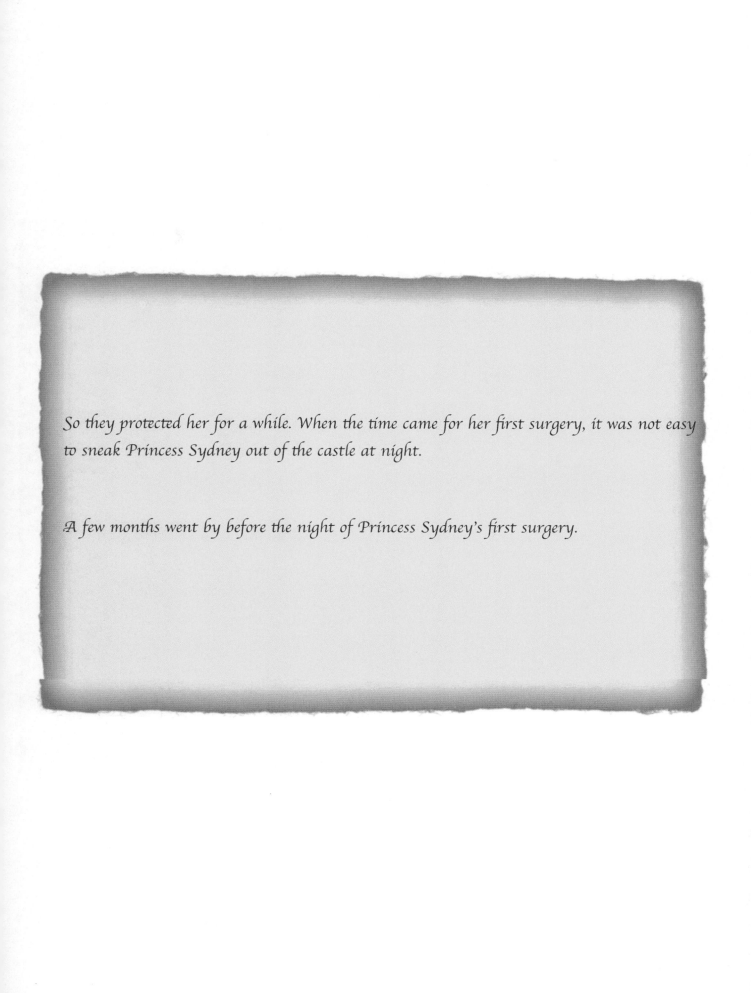

So they protected her for a while. When the time came for her first surgery, it was not easy to sneak Princess Sydney out of the castle at night.

A few months went by before the night of Princess Sydney's first surgery.

While riding along the road to the hospital, they saw a person on the side of the road. "Slow down" ordered the King to the horseman. "I think that is Father Alex. He has fallen." said the King to the Queen. "Please horseman, stop!" he begged; "we must help him!"

"Father Alex!" yelled the King. "We are here to help you!"

"Thank you," said Father Alex. "I was walking to the hospital to help the sick when I tripped over a branch. I will be fine, thank you for stopping."

"Well, Father Alex," said the King, "today is your lucky day, we are heading to the hospital ourselves and we can take you the rest of the way."

"Oh! That would be wonderful," said Father Alex. "Wait! Are you ok?"

"Yes Father, we are bringing our daughter to have surgery."

Father Alex said, "Well since we are headed over there, I will pray and give a blessing to the Princess."

"Thank you, Father Alex," said the King.

"Hello Queen, may I see the child?"

The Queen nervously replied, "Yes, Father."

Father Alex looked at the princess and says "OHH MYYY!"

The King and Queen held their breath then gasped.

"She is so Beautiful! What a sight to see! Here is her blessing and she will do wonderfully."

The King was shocked and said, "I know that she looks different Father. Please don't speak to anyone about the Princess."

Father Alex replied, "Don't worry my son but it is a shame you are keeping this beautiful child away from the Kingdom."

"Thank you Father, but I feel the Kingdom will not accept her because she is different."

Father replied, "King, God made us all different and beautiful in our own way. Princess Sydney's eyes shine with the love you and the Queen give her. The Kingdom will not only accept her, they will love her too."

A few weeks later the King told the Queen, "We shall present Princess Sydney to the Kingdom on her first birthday."

The Queen replied, "Are you sure? The Princess still has more surgeries coming up and she still looks different."

"Yes!" said the King, "after talking to Father Alex I believe the Kingdom will love her as one of their own."

So when the day of Princess Sydney's first birthday arrived, they readied to present her to the Kingdom of Resilience.

The royal trumpets sounded, to announce the King and Queen.

"To the people of Resilience, I present to you your Princess."

The crowd chanted with anticipation.

The royal trumpets sounded again.

"Princess Sydney Strong!"

"At first you hear a loud gasp...."

"Then a bigger cheer and celebration came from the crowd."

The King and Queen were very happy.

Then they noticed Princess Sydney waiving to the crowd and smiling.

The Queen looked at the King and says, "We got a $\underline{\mathrm{Smart}}$ one on our hands."

The King replied, "Just like her mother."

As Sydney continued to grow and have surgeries, she had the love and support of her family and the people of Resilience.

One day, as the Princess was playing with her many toys, she asked her mom. "Mom, why do I have so many toys? I know I can't play with all of them."

"Well honey," said the Queen, "the people of the Kingdom want to show you the love and support they have for you."

Princess Sydney replied, "Well mom, is there any chance we can give a few toys to the other children of the Kingdom who don't have toys?"

"Wow!" says the Queen, "What a great and <u>Caring</u> idea!"

The Queen told the King about the idea.

So they decided to build a play center for all the kids of the Kingdom to play with Princess Sydney and all her toys.

This made Princess Sydney very happy and she saw the importance of caring for others.

Now that the new play center was open, Princess Sydney started to make new friends.

Princess Sydney Strong Play Center

A
Place to Be Yourself

P SS

It was a little strange at first because the boys and girls in the kingdom would stare at Princess Sydney and would ask why her eyes look different.

Princess Sydney, being so smart and caring, decided to do something funny each time she met someone new.

You see, she wanted to make them feel ok to be around her, even though she looked different.

She would wave hello first with a big smile. If the boy or girl waved and smiled back, she would bring them in and show them around the play center.

If the wave hello didn't work, she would ask them if they had any questions. Although she knew they had the one question in their mind.

They would ask, "Why do your eyes look so different?"

She would reply, "Well, I was born this way, but I will let you in on a secret. Because my eyes are so big, I can see from here to the other side of the Kingdom."

This would make the children laugh and forget how different she looked.

The King would tell the Queen, "We have a Funny one on our hands."

The Queen would reply, "Just like her father."

As the years went by and Princess Sydney had more surgeries, the Kingdom spread the word about Princess Sydney and told the other kingdoms how <u>Brave</u> and <u>Strong</u> she was for going to see the doctor and having to go through so many surgeries.

There was one surgery that made the King and Queen very nervous.

Sydney was reaching an age that would require her to wear a special device called a Halo.

Princess Sydney would have to wear the Halo on her head and face for a few months.

This was the surgery that would make Princess Sydney the bravest and strongest princess of all the kingdoms in the world.

It would take the King and Queen, with the help of all of the Kingdom, to help Princess Sydney and to believe she was going to get through it.

The day of the surgery the kingdom made signs for Princess Sydney saying they Believe in her and love her very much.

The King and Queen were so touched by the show of support, they promised everyone a great celebration when Princess Sydney removed her Halo.

Then the King and Queen, with tears in their eyes, remembered the day Father Alex told them the Kingdom would not only accept Princess Sydney but they would also love her as one of their own.

As Sydney recovered from her surgery for the next few months, the word about Princess Sydney continued to spread around the kingdoms.

Finally, the day came when Princess Sydney had her Halo removed.

As promised by the King and Queen, a big celebration was put together with the whole kingdom invited....

With one very special surprise from the Royal Knights of Resilience.

The royal trumpets sounded, "I am Sir Perseverance! The leader of the Royal Knights of Resilience. We have heard of your stories of bravery and strength and would like to honor you and your family with this award for being the Bravest and Strongest Princess of all the kingdoms of the world."

All the knights bowed down to Princess Sydney Strong, and Sir Perseverance handed her the award.

Princess Sydney thanked the knights and told everyone in the Kingdom,

"I could not have done this alone. My Mother and Father have given me the love and support that only parents could give."

"The people of Resilience have also given me the love and support that only a kingdom could give."

"I am very thankful and would like to share with you what makes me different. I would like for all of you and especially the children to repeat after me."

I am Beautiful.

I am Smart.

I am Funny.

I am Caring.

I am Brave.

I am Strong.

And

I Believe in Me.

"I repeat this to myself every day. I do this to remind myself of what you have all taught me throughout my life."

"The most important part of all of this, is you all believed in me so much that I started to believe in myself."

"Thank you for such a great gift."

The King and Queen could not have been any prouder of their Princess, so they decreed that all the children would practice saying Princess Sydney's mantra every day at school.

The End

Princess Sydney's story does not end here.

It's just the beginning.

Made in the USA
Middletown, DE
31 August 2019